All the New
Tomorrows

5 Science Fiction Stories

REBECCA M. SENESE

OTHER BOOKS BY REBECCA M. SENESE

Mind Hunt

The Soul Within

Tales of Possibilities: 10 Science Fiction Stories

Future Visions: 5 Science Fiction Stories

Evacuation Day

Moon Dream

Download Complete

Who Do You Think You Are?

Rite to Life

The Beyond Saga:
Beyond Control, Interlude, Beyond Reach
Beyond Bounds
Beyond Limits

All the New Tomorrows

5 Science Fiction Stories

Rebecca M. Senese

RFAR Publishing
Toronto, Canada

Published 2014 by RFAR Publishing
Toronto, Canada
http://www.RFARPublishing.com

This is a work of fiction. All characters appearing in this work are fictitious. Any resemblance to real persons, living or dear is purely coincidental.

Trade paper edition designed by Rebecca M. Senese
in InDesign CS5.5

Electronic editions designed by Rebecca M. Senese

Cover design: Rebecca M. Senese
Cover Image © pschubert / MorgueFile.com
Interior Images © alisher / CanStockPhoto.com
cidepix / CanStockPhoto.com

ISBN: 978-1-927603-21-5

Publications Acknowledgement

"Brothers Under the Skin." First published in *Storyteller*, 2006.

"Cold War" won second prize in the *X the Unknown Anthology* contest, 1998. Published in the *Dark Tales Anthology*, 2005

"Face Dances." First published in *On Spec*, 1996 and reprinted in the anthology *Future Syndicate*, 2007.

"I of the Beholder." First published in *Oddlands Magazine*, 2008.

"Reawakening." First published in *Storyteller*, 2002.

All the New Tomorrows

Tomorrows

5 Science Fiction Stories

TABLE OF CONTENTS

INTRODUCTION

Welcome to my *All the New Tomorrows* compilation. I've always loved science fiction, ever since I watched Star Trek while sitting on my mother's lap. For me, the best science fiction isn't just about exploring strange worlds but about exploring what it means to be human, how we define ourselves and each other and how the world around us effects those expectations and experiences.

In these stories, characters explore their world and their place inside it. Will they be happy with what they find? How will that world affect them? I invite you to explore with them.

Enjoy!

Rebecca M. Senese
December 2013

Brothers Under The Skin

Occasionally she would slip and call him "David."

At first it confused him; his name was Tommy. He'd learned that quickly; he was a bright boy. She called him Tommy most of the time but occasionally she would slip and the word "David" would come out and when he looked confused, she would become angry. But her anger dissolved quickly into guilty tears and she would bend down to hug him so tight he could barely breathe.

Once when he was six he asked who David was. Daddy got angry, a pinched look crossing his face. He slammed the newsreader shut and left the dining room without a word. Mommy clenched her coffee cup and her teeth. When he looked at her she snapped at him to finish his breakfast.

Her angry tone upset him, made him want to cry but he was a big boy now and big boys didn't cry. With a sniff, he bent over his cereal.

He never asked about David again.

The teasing started when he went to junior high school.

He never knew how they found out but they did. It wasn't so bad that they knew, it was that they knew before he did.

Gregory Martin was the first one. All fat muscle over a bullish temperament, he ambled over at lunch.

"Hey little clone," he sneered. "Who are you?"

When he started to laugh, all the other kids joined in.

Shame reddened Tommy's cheeks even through his confusion. Clone? What was he talking about? Then Tommy recalled his mother's face, flushed with shame and residual pain.

David.

He stayed after school that night to access the library. He could have used his home terminal but the school's was generic and although he had to use his school ident card, it didn't prove he used the computer. Everybody traded ident cards in school. It was a way to access more than you were supposed to. The school knew about it but couldn't stop it.

One of his friends had shown him how to access government records just a few days ago. With a few tricks, you could slip through the defenses and look at whatever you wanted. Tommy hunched over the hand reader and steered along.

He knew he'd been born at Mercy Memorial Hospital. Finding the hospital didn't take very long but he had to wade through the current admissions before he could get through to archives. There now. His tongue pressed against the top of his teeth. Birth records, finally.

Scrolling back took a long time, but he didn't want to miss it. As it was, he almost did.

There, born October 21st, 2097. Thomas Dreyford, cross reference 970214.

Cross reference? What was that? He clicked on the reference and waited.

A moment later a file sprang open, including a picture. Tommy stared at his own face. His borrowed face. He stared for a full twenty minutes before he could look at the name.

David Thomas Dreyford.

He copied the file without reading anymore. He couldn't read anymore right now. God it was late, mom would kill him. His hands shook as he stuffed the bubble-mem into his knapsack.

His mind stayed blank on the speedtrain ride home.

"You look a little pale, Tommy. Are you all right?" Mom said when he walked into the living room.

"I'm just tired. I think I'll lie down before dinner."

He turned away to avoid her reply and retreated to his bedroom.

Dimming the window shield, Tommy laid down on the bed. He felt heavy, as though he could sink into his mattress and break through the floor. Then he would sink through the rest of the house and into the ground until he reached the hot, molten core of the earth.

He was a clone. The thought created a tiny ripple on the surface of his mind. He could feel it moving outward, gaining strength. Soon it would become a tidal wave, growing to engulf him. He would drown in himself.

His fingers itched to open the knapsack but he didn't trust himself. Not yet.

Mom's voice drifted up the stairwell, calling him to dinner. He knew if he didn't answer she'd use the com system even though she hated it.

He waited.

Sure enough the speaker by the door crackled. She could never get it to work right.

"Tommy? Come down for dinner." Her voice dissolved in a burst of static.

"Voice reply," he said. "I'm not hungry. I don't feel like eating."

More static. "Do you feel okay?"

He didn't reply. What could he say? He wasn't quite sure what he felt.

A few minutes later she knocked on the door and used her override to open it.

"Tommy?"

"Yeah."

"Windows, forty percent light," she said. The darkness slowly lightened into gloom. He could see her body silhouetted against the doorway. He wanted to cry out to her, ask her before he had to see it for himself. Ask her just once to be honest.

Then she moved and the moment was lost.

"Do you feel sick?" she asked. She moved to stand by the bed and put her hand on his forehead. Her skin was cool and soft.

"I'm just not hungry," he said.

"You do feel a little hot," she said. "You keep resting. I'll bring you up some soup."

"Maybe later."

"Okay, later."

Her hand stroked off his forehead and ruffled his bangs. As her fingers slipped away, he bit his lip to stop the tears. His mother reached the door and without turning back, called, "Windows dark."

If she turned as the door closed, he didn't see it as the light slowly faded to black.

While his parents slept, he took out the disk and with trembling fingers, slipped it into his computer. His finger hovered over the access key.

Why are you doing this? he asked himself. Just because Gregory Martin, who was the biggest asshole ever to rumble down the hallways of Everston Junior High sneered at him? Martin sneered at everyone, gunning for the slightest vulnerability. It didn't mean a damn thing.

But it did. He knew it. It explained a lot of things.

Things as simple as his mother calling him a different name and his father unable to look him in the eye. He'd thought that was just the way it was, but now he saw it was only surface. The truth lay beneath the waves.

He pressed the access button. The truth washed over him and filled his mouth, his nose, his ears until he thought he would die drowning.

David Thomas Dreyford. Born October 21st, 2089, died February 12th, 2097. No murdered

February 12th, 2097. Genetic samples taken for cloning on February 14th, 2097. Implantation into Marion Helen Dreyford, February 15th, 2097.

Tommy had to search most of the night before he found the trial records of one Mathew Hendrix, age twenty-nine, convicted of the sexual assault and murder of seven young boys including David Thomas Dreyford. Many of the specifics were missing including Hendrix's own testimony blanked out behind an impenetrable barrier.

Unplugging at four in the morning, he sat in the darkness, feeling the waves move within him, slowly dissolving the layers of his mind. He wasn't really a person, wasn't really unique. A copy, made by grieving parents. Why couldn't they at least give him the dignity of telling him the truth?

That day he told his mother he was ill and stayed home from school.

She fussed a little, wanting to stay home with him but he insisted he would sleep most of the day. Finally she relented, leaving him with direct access to her cellphone if he needed it.

He actually did try to sleep, but couldn't. Thoughts drifted in his mind like sharks, nipping away at pieces of him.

He wasn't real. Nothing he had done was his own. A sudden thought seized him. Had they raised David the same way?

The idea propelled him out of bed and up to the attic where mother stored their "history" or "junk" as Dad called it.

Dust had settled on everything, despite the ventilator. Tommy coughed as he ripped open boxes, poring through old clothing and real paper books. Finally in a corner under a support beam, he found a black chest packed with boy's clothes. Beneath the clothes he dug up some holo pictures. His own face stared back, young, joyous, dressed in a hockey uniform. No, not his face. David's.

They'd made Tommy play hockey too.

He dug deeper and deeper. Books, titles he knew, clothes similar to his own. Not his, not him. Everything in the trunk, packed neatly and nicely away, they'd recreated for him. As if he wasn't his own person, just a copy.

Just a clone.

Stifling a sob, he slammed the trunk shut. He was a clone. He didn't exist. A cheap copy of David. The books he'd read, the toys he'd played with, the hockey team he'd joined, none of it his, all of it David's. David's.

In the end, he took only his knapsack, crammed with his hand computer and as many ultima-sized bubble-mem as he thought he could sell. Everything else belonged to someone else's life. He left it behind. He checked his watch, two o'clock. He could be out of the city before they got home.

He locked the door after him and disconnected his voice access. He took a speedtrain to the station and hopped onto the next shuttle out.

They would probably look for him but he wondered who they were really looking for. A boy dead almost fifteen years. It was time they accepted it.

The bubble-chips sold as easily as he thought but the money didn't last, especially when he got his first taste of Planet X.

He remembered it vividly. Sitting in a burned out condo with Vicki J and her man Edmund.

They'd bought his last three bubble-chips for a reasonable price.

"Here, have a taste of this," Vicki J purred. She was twenty but looked fifty. Tommy thought she was worldly.

Edmund, lounging in the corner, flashed his silver-striped teeth. The additional inner row hung lower giving him a shark expression and making it impossible for him to completely close his jaw.

Vicki J held out what looked like a licorice stick. With a smile, she licked her lips, holding the stick to Tommy's mouth. The look of her lips excited him. He opened his mouth and sucked.

The waves in his mind swirled and bubbled. Soon they were dissolving away in a rush of steam. Everything dissolved, the squalid room, Edmund's silver teeth, Vicki J's thick lips. His parents rushed into his mind and they too dissolved. Everything melted until there was nothing left. Nothing left.

But David.

Then David too began to dissolve. Clouds of billowing steam obscured his boyish face, melted his fine hair. Finally there was nothing, nothing at all.

Tommy fell in love with nothing.

The money went quickly after that. The waves in Tommy's mind focused only on one thing, getting more Planet X. It was the only way he could truly empty his mind of David. The only chance he had of creating himself.

He tried soliciting but even at fourteen, he was too old for most of the customers who trolled in the southside of the city. Occasionally he got a lookout job but as the police began to recognize him his usefulness deteriorated.

All his money went to Planet X. He barely ate now, his clothes hung off him. He kept them clean, had to, never know when there'd be work and he'd have to look good. Or at least alive.

Finally one of the regulars approached him. He was a big guy, the others called him Mean Freddy and whispered about what he did. He wore a smile like a leer and draped an arm across Tommy's shoulders.

"You know, you're a looker," Mean Freddy said. "I like them blue eyes."

"Two," Tommy said. "Three and we can spend the night."

Mean Freddy chuckled. "Not like that. You're too old for me. But you could fetch me some little ones."

Mean Freddy paid for a haircut and a shower and sent him to one of the schools in the north end. He'd promised five on delivery, enough for almost four weeks worth of Planet X.

Tommy sat on a bench across from the school, watching the kids trail out on their way home. The waves in his mind were moving again, drowning everything inside. Disgust, guilt, longing, fear. This intensity made him think of David and filled him with rage. It was too much. He had to have the nothing, had to erase everything, only then could he rebuild, he told himself.

Finally the flow of kids trickled away to one, a boy, hauling a gym bag. Stayed late for practice, football or something, Tommy thought. He stood up to follow the boy.

He caught up at the next lights.

"Blasters fan," he said.

The boy jerked, startled. He looked over at Tommy. "Yeah."

"They need better runners," Tommy said. He turned to face the boy, showing how young he was himself.

The boy, no older than nine, relaxed a little. "Yeah, their runners suck." A little grin touched his lips. Talking tough to the older kid.

"Yeah," Tommy agreed. "You any good?" He gestured at the gym bag.

"First cut," said the boy.

"Great. What's your name?"

"Jason. What's yours?"

Tommy smiled as the waves rolled in his mind. "My name's David," he said. "Wanna walk home?"

The boy shrugged. Tommy took the boy's gym bag and hoisted it to his shoulder.

The light turned green and they crossed, walking farther into the darkness where the waves would stir no more.

Cold War

After the cops left, taking Wilson's wasted corpse, Pete was still shaky from panic. So close, goddammit, too close.

When they'd rung the buzzer at five that morning, snarling into the vid-cam, he was sure they'd come for him.

Spike ratted, he'd thought wildly as his trembling fingers fumbled on the door lock keypad. The cops waved piercer guns, powerful enough to blast through a three inch steel door, never mind the thin slice of plexiwood that was the apartment door.

Some damn high security building, Pete thought.

Finally his fingers cooperated, punching in the code. The door inched open then swung wide as one of the cops kicked it. The shiny, ominous end of a split-fire, twenty-five round, piercer gun jammed under Pete's nose. The smell of oil and death nearly choked him.

"Wilson?" snarled the cop. "Bunter Wilson?"

Pete blinked in surprise. He pointed across the narrow six foot apartment. Wilson cowered against the wall, emaciated shoulders scraping peeling paint. Bony fingers clutched the sheet. Glazed eyes stared out in fear beneath thinning blond hair.

The cop pushed Pete away and three of them strolled into the room. A lieutenant wearing a shapeless black overcoat and armored gloves opened a leather case. He glanced at the contents and back at Wilson.

"Bunter Wilson, you are charged with skipping your six month test," the lieutenant said. His voice grated from too many herbal cigarettes. "As such a blood test is to be administered immediately. Having skipped the test, you have no right to legal counsel and any conclusion drawn from the following blood test is deemed valid and admissible in court."

He drew out a thin pencil-like object. The tester. A nod to the other cops sent them gliding forward. Wilson didn't bother to struggle as they held out his arm.

Pete had heard of cases where the blood tests were wrong. Fat lot of good that did the poor jerks who had to take them.

Wilson flinched as the tester beeped once and lit up. Red. The lieutenant's face was glacial.

"Bunter Wilson, you have tested positive. Your twenty-four hour amnesty period has been waived due to your non compliance with the law."

Pocketing the tester, the lieutenant pulled out a twister wand and jabbed it at Wilson's chest. As the wand touched him, the cops let go and Wilson's body quivered, jerking to the rhythm of the lethal dose of electricity. The smell of cooked flesh filled the air. Pete gagged.

Wilson's body flopped to the floor when the

lieutenant switched the wand off. One hand lay, palm up, dirty fingernails pointing at the ceiling as if beseeching mercy from an uncaring god.

Without glancing at him, the lieutenant left, mumbling about paperwork, leaving the heavily armored cops to carry Wilson. They picked him up unceremoniously and dragged the body out of the apartment.

Pete scurried into his biker leathers, the stench of Wilson's passing still strong and rank in the air. He had to get the hell out before the cleanup crew arrived. They were supposed to come with the cops and look for any contraband on the premises, but things rarely went the way they were supposed to. Witness Wilson.

If they found Pete here he'd be screwed. Totally. No telling what they had on him already.

Three blocks away the familiar white van streaked past, heading for the apartment building. Pete ducked his head so they wouldn't get a good look at his face. Too damn close. Just his luck to find a roomie who wasn't a health freak or an organ hunter only to have the cops waste him. A skipper, who woulda thought that about Wilson?

He aimed down Yonge Street, the early morning air stinking of sewage and pollution wafting north from the poisoned lake. Although he knew it was too early to make contact he was going to do it anyway. Things around here were getting too hot too fast. No telling what the cleanup crew would uncover. The apartment had been in Wilson's name and Pete had been very careful about not letting anything slip but it would be noticed that he hadn't stayed for the debriefing. Noticed and reported.

Time to collect his stash and blow this town.

Angling down York Street, he hit Queens Quay. Around him, the buildings of a bygone era reached up for the sky, as pathetic as Wilson's hand. After the lake poisoning, the rich had fled from their luxury condominiums and gangs of squatters had taken over. Not even the police came this far south.

The stench was bad so he pulled out a face-filter. It was an old one, but he hadn't been paid for the last shipment yet. With the apartment gone, he didn't know how Spike would contact him.

The heaviness of the sewage crept through his worn filter. At least it was bearable. He adjusted the strap over his crooked nose. Seals never closed properly around it.

A dull, yellow sun glared down as Pete circled the buildings. He couldn't see anybody but he knew better. The gangs were watching; he could feel their eyes the way he could feel a custom inspector's suspicions. They wouldn't touch him yet though. Not with the red handkerchief of the Hapslam gang tied around his right arm.

It was dangerous to be this early but there wasn't anywhere else to go. His hands still trembled, remembering Wilson's death dance. He had to get his stash now.

Finally a figure appeared against one of the ruined doorways. Swathed in rags, it glided towards him across the barren parking lot. Only when it got within six feet could Pete tell it was a woman.

"Where's Matrix?" Pete said. He didn't need this right now.

"He got caught yesterday, up around Rosedale. Tested positive."

Pete closed his eyes. Oh great. Now what? If Spike found out he lost a shipment, running from the cops would be the least of his worries. Spike was increasingly nervous about the crackdown on her smugglers. Too many of them had turned or just plain disappeared.

"I'm your contact now." The woman's voice broke into his thoughts.

He opened his eyes to study her, or what he could see of her. Deep brown eyes stared out at him over a filter mask that looked even older than his. Tufts of black hair peeked out from the rags wrapped like a turban around her head. Impossible to see the shape of her body under the various pieces of fabric covering her.

"Who the hell are you?" Pete demanded. He patted his left thigh where the thin plasti-wire knife rested. She was small, but he knew how vicious these homeless could be. He wanted her to know he wasn't intimated by her.

"I'm Vriana," she said. "Matrix's daughter."

Pete pursed his lips. Matrix had never mentioned a daughter, but they'd never swapped life stories. Mostly business, which was how Pete liked it. No attachments, no losses.

"Where's my stuff?"

"It's safe," she said. Pete waited, but she merely stared at him.

"Look, I can't pay you now. You get paid when I get paid. I have to make delivery."

Her dark eyes narrowed. "This isn't about money. I want to meet your lead. We want an adjustment to the arrangement."

Shit, he didn't need this now. "What kind of adjustment?"

"I'm not discussing it with you, just your lead."

"Give me my stuff first." His fingers itched to unfasten the plasti-wire knife cover but violence was the wrong way to respond. He didn't underestimate her.

Apparently she didn't underestimate him either. Her gaze barely flickered from his face but she took a shuffling step back.

"Are we going to stalemate?" she said. "Matrix said you were smarter than that."

He was smarter and at the moment, hungry. Hell,

so they wanted to meet Spike, what did he care? He was a middleman, he didn't care about agreements.

"Food first," he said.

He was grateful she didn't tell him what was in the stew. As they squatted by the fire in the lobby of an old condominium complex, he snuck glances at her over the edge of his cracked bowl. Without the filter mask, he could see the resemblance to Matrix in her face; the long nose, the high cheekbones. Her dark eyes contrasted her father's blue ones, but they held the same expression, hard and intense.

"You got my stuff on you?" Pete asked casually.

Vriana shot him an amused look. "Hurry up."

Before they left, she exchanged her homeless robes for the chic patched leathers and mock furs of a fake slummer. The vertical stripes accentuated her slim waist, curving her hips even more. With an effort, Pete looked at her face. Her brown eyes were steely. He didn't want to know how she'd acquired such an expensive outfit.

"Move," she said.

He led her up York Street to Queen where they headed west. He removed the red band from his arm and stuffed it in a pocket. The kid gangs here didn't appreciate homeless affiliations. Vriana studied the street and the barricaded store fronts. She's probably never been this far north, Pete realized.

He zagged up Spadina and spent time wandering around the decrepit shops.

Vriana glared at him. "How much longer?" she asked.

"As long as it takes," he said. He ignored her scowl. He had to make sure they weren't being followed.

Finally they ducked in the back way to Massey College. He steered her past the tables, loaded with black market merchandise and upstairs.

"You smuggle all that?" she asked.

He glanced down the stairs, at the row of fresh fruit, the meager stacks of blank paper, and the folded clothes guaranteed to contain no tracer threads.

"Not all, but some."

At a thick oak door, he stopped and knocked

once. A few moments passed. Vriana shifted impatiently from foot to foot. She blinked rapidly. Pete suppressed a smile; she probably didn't even realize she was being scanned.

The door opened, granting them admittance. Spike, sitting behind a dark mahogany desk, waved them in. Her scuffed leather boots rested on the desk's elegant top.

"I don't give a shit what he says," Spike shouted into the phone. "Make sure." She slammed down the receiver and ran one wrinkled hand through her gray streaked hair.

"Hello Pete," she said amiably. "Tell me why you've brought me some homeless tramp and not my shipment."

She was in a bad mood. The more Spike smiled, the angrier she was, and right now she was positively beaming. Great day, Pete thought, and it wasn't even noon yet.

"My holder was lost in a Rosedale sweep," he said. "She says she's got the shipment and wants to talk to you."

Thankfully, Spike's scathing gaze turned to Vriana. "And what do you want?"

Vriana didn't even flinch. "We want to review the terms of our agreement."

"Your terms are more than generous and not open for negotiation."

Vriana smiled coldly. "We know you deal with other homeless gangs. You won't just lose one shipment if you refuse to talk."

Spike leisurely cupped her hands behind her head. Pete winced; was Matrix's daughter stupid or just plain blind?

"You homeless aren't the only game in town," Spike purred. "We have options."

"You won't even listen to our terms?" Vriana said. Interesting change of tactics, Pete thought.

Spike shrugged as if she didn't care either way.

"It's a better deal than you have now," Vriana continued. "We hold your shipments for you and instead of paying in cash, we'll take equipment. At a generous turnaround for you."

Spike dropped her arms and leaned forward. "What kind of equipment?"

Vriana said nothing, but it started to fall together for Pete. Everything he'd ever seen out at Harbourfront pointed to it. Matrix and his books, the desperate methods they used to erase ident markers and discourage police from patrolling the area.

"Laboratory," Pete said.

Vriana cursed and glared at him. Spike's look was quizzical.

"The homeless can get any kind of weapon," he said. "Anybody can with the right amount of money, but laboratory equipment is something else."

"What the hell do you want with that?" Spike asked.

"What do you think?" Vriana snapped. "Hasn't it occurred to you what they're doing? They're infecting us all and we have to find a way to stop it."

Spike rubbed one leathery cheek. "Why would I want to stop it?"

Vriana sputtered. "Why? What? How can you...?"

"Why," Spike continued, "would I want to stop something that makes me so much money? That pays for a market like the one downstairs? Things could be a lot worse."

"Worse!" Vriana shouted. "What could be worse?"

"Dead for one," Spike said. "If even it were suspected that I gave you the equipment you want..." She shrugged at the inevitable.

"You won't deal, you don't get your shipment. Not this one or any other."

"Fine," Spike said, rubbing her nose.

Shit, Pete thought. The kill signal. Bad idea. The homeless pursued their grudges with a vengeance and killing Matrix's daughter could lead to a war. From the look on Spike's face he knew if he didn't do it, he'd be dead. So he did what he always did when faced with an impossible situation.

Fake incompetence.

He reached for the plasti-wire knife, deliberately shifting his right foot to draw Vriana's attention. He allowed her another second as he drew the blade, then there was no turning back. If she didn't realize what was happening he'd have to kill her.

The blade came free, humming in his hand. He struck with his left hand. Immediately, she pivoted, hand flashing down. Pain spazmed in

Pete's forearm and he allowed the knife to drop. Vriana didn't follow through as he expected but whirled on Spike.

"Is this how you deal with your contractors?"

"No," Spike said. "This is."

She pulled out a pistol and fired.

Pete rolled, knocking Vriana's legs out from under her. She collapsed on top of him, the shot zinging over her head. Pete mumbled curses under his breath; could this possibly get any worse?

Vriana twisted, pulling something from her pant's pocket. With a snap, she flung it up in the air as Spike stood to get a better angle. Vriana's hand clamped over Pete's eyes, but didn't entirely protect them from the blast.

He heard Spike's strangled cry and a thump. When Vriana released him, he climbed to his feet. Spike lay crumpled behind her desk.

"A light shock wave," Vriana said. "She'll be out for a while." She studied him curiously. "Why did you warn me?"

"Call me stupid," Pete said.

"Looks like you're out of a job," she said. "Want a new one?"

He turned to look at her. Her dark hair was tousled in a mess around her thin face, the fake furs around her shoulders askew. She looked normal, just like anybody else.

"You're infected, right?"

She bobbed her head. "Most of us are. It's burning us out, the older ones are really bad off. But you'll know that soon enough."

He blinked at her stupidly. "Huh?"

"I'm sorry, Pete. You're infected now too."

"What the hell do you mean it's a cold?"

Vriana shook her head. Dark hair swayed. The neon lights in the mall made it glint.

But Pete wasn't interested. Here he'd risked his job for her only to find out he was infected. Just great.

"That's how it's spread," she whispered. She threw a glance at the shops. It was an upper-class mall, she'd probably never been in one before, Pete realized. He tried to remember what he thought when he'd seen the regulated shops, the healthy upper classes walking around in their designer style-of-life suits with matching air filters and oxygen tanks. Never saw their faces, only the masks.

"You don't have a cold," he said.

She reached into a pocket and pulled out several white capsules. "Decongestants."

Pete turned away to watch a couple walk by, their masks decorated with garish strips of colour and bits of metal welded on. The latest fashion.

"We're inside," Vriana said. "Don't they ever take those masks off?"

"No," Pete said. He took hold of her elbow and steered her away from the gang of upper classes she was staring at. "The virus?"

"Oh right. We think the purpose is to clean the organs out of waste products."

"What's wrong with that?"

"What's wrong is it burns people out. And some have been disappearing."

"Yeah, the testing," Pete said.

Vriana shook her head. "No, not killed. Disappeared. We think they're harvesting the organs for transplants."

Pete stared at her. She looked serious. So that's what this was about, the request for equipment.

Weapons they could get aplenty, but lab equipment was something else. Probably wanted to develop some kind of vaccine or something.

"We need that equipment," Vriana said. "You could..."

"No, I can't do anything," Pete said. "I'm finished here. I got friends in South Am, they aren't so strict down there. Maybe I'll pick coffee beans or something. You can do whatever you want."

She looked about to protest but Pete motioned toward the exit.

"I think we've shaken any tails. I'll take you home."

The sun was bleeding across the horizon in a sunset that reminded Pete of vomit when they hit Queen's Quay. The familiar homeless buildings stretched in front of them. Pete frowned and slowed down. Some kind of transport was parked in front of one of the buildings. A thin vein of smoke drifted out of the buildings' front door.

"Cops," Vriana hissed just as a concussion grenade came whizzing toward them.

Pete grabbed her arm and threw her back. The grenade exploded, sending shockwaves through his system. Pete's brain felt scrambled. His skin tingled. Angry shouts filled his ears.

Time to get out. Pete forced his aching body to move. Nerves screamed as he climbed to his feet. The shouting got louder and now he could hear the pounding of armoured boots. He grabbed Vriana's arm, trying to drag her to her feet. Through drifting smoke he caught a flash of a swiftly moving figure.

Getting closer.

"Come on," he shouted, stumbling a couple of steps, still pulling Vriana's arm. She was moving now, slowly rising to her feet. One hand fumbled with the buckle on her belt. It dropped to the ground. Then with a surge of sudden strength, she raced past Pete, this time dragging him in her wake.

He didn't look back as he ran. The flash lighten Vriana's hair, sending a long shadow racing out in front of her. The wind came a moment later, its force propelling Pete even faster. A personal nuke, he realized. Shit, the homeless were well equipped.

Hadn't done them much good.

They kept running until Pete's lungs felt like they were going to burst. Gasping, he grabbed Vriana's arm and dragged her to a halt. She tried to pull away and Pete noticed the panic on her face, the way her eyes darted wildly. Poor kid, he thought, first her father, now her whole community. But he couldn't let her freak out, they had to keep their wits.

"Where you going?" he snapped. "Get your mind in gear. I don't have time for bullshit hysterics."

She stared at him a moment, eyes still wild, then anger crossed her face like a cloud. It brought her back to herself, just like he intended.

"You bastard," she snarled but he stopped her with a raised hand.

"You're right, I'm not going to argue the point," he said. "But unless you've got an idea, running like that will only attract attention."

The way her head drooped told him she was listening. Good, maybe their asses weren't cooked. Yet.

So now what would he do with her? Leave her behind? Even as he thought the words, he knew he couldn't do it. Matrix had always been a fair contact. Not a friend; Pete didn't have friends, couldn't afford them. But if he had, he would have liked one like Matrix, maybe even one like this intense woman standing before him.

Pete sniffed, rubbing his nose. His sinuses were clogging up and he could feel the beginnings of a headache pound out a rhythm in his temples. Just great. But it did give him a thought.

"I have an idea," he said. "Some place the cops would never think of looking."

Granny hadn't stopped wiping his hands with a handkerchief since they walked in, Pete noticed. He'd ushered them immediately into a small room off the foyer entrance as if their mere presence would pollute the apartment's atmosphere. The bay window in the room faced east, showing the glow from the Pickering Nuclear Plant. Granny stood there now, his tall, skeletal form awash in fabric. Beady eyes stared out from behind thick glasses. He glanced at Vriana and wiped his hands.

"What do you want, Peter?" His voice held all the tension of a man being force to do something distasteful.

Too damned bad, Pete thought.

"I need information and passage," he said and then sneezed.

Granny frowned, thin lips etching an ugly line across his face. "I don't know..."

Pete pulled out a rumpled rag and rubbed his nose. "I do," he said softly. "I know lots."

Granny stiffened, posture ramrod straight and so tight Pete thought Granny's spine would snap.

"You know I wouldn't be here if it wasn't important," Pete said.

The man sagged, nodding, looking even more glum. He wiped his hands one last time and stuffed the handkerchief in the pocket of his flowing jacket.

"Talk," he grunted at Pete.

Pete talked. Wilson, the stash, Vriana, Spike, the cops. Vriana scowled when he spoke about the homeless's virus theory but Pete knew he had to tell everything. Granny would sense a left out piece.

By the end, Granny's thin face was crinkled with amusement. "Transplants, eh?" he challenged Vriana. She stared back at him, fists clenched.

"I can see how you thought that." He nodded absently to himself. He turned toward the window, eyes defocusing. Pete tensed in anticipation. Info dump.

"Virus adaptus they called it in the lab, a joke name for a not so humourous disease. It does clean out the organs, but more than that. Adaptation, regulation, genetic manipulation from the inside out. The testing confirms the effectiveness of the virus, green for uninfected, red for mutation, yellow for appropriate adaptation."

"If not transplantation," Vriana said, "then what?"

She'd spoken before Pete could stop her. He glared at her, silencing her next question. Her answering glare told him she didn't know what was going on but he couldn't explain now. Pete held up his hand to entreat her not to say another word.

But Granny didn't seem to have heard.

"Harvesting is completed at an early stage and the yellows are brought in for further conditioning," he continued. "Reds are destroyed because of possible transmittal of the mutant strain. Greens are left alone and may never be infected. In this way, they can ensure a specific type for transportation off-world."

Pete bit his tongue to stop from speaking. His headache pounded across his skull like a drumbeat. This was always the hardest part, waiting for the info dump to finish. Usually he could be patient, but this cold was a constant reminder that his life as he'd known it was over and he was desperate for answers. But interrupting could be fatal to the reader and there were no better readers than Granny.

"Labor camps," the thin man announced. "Off-world camps unsuitable for non-adapted humans. That's why the genetic reconfiguration as well as neural shut down of all upper mind functions. The virus begins the process internally but external physical mutation and erasure of neural processes must be done in the lab. Everything not related to obedience and work is erased."

Vriana's face, pale to begin with, blanched white beneath her dark hair. Pete imagined he had the same haunted look. What was he now, a red, a yellow? What was she?

He waited another moment but Granny was finished. Slowly the man came back, blinking, hands fluttering amongst the folds of fabric. After a deep breath, he shook his head.

"Nothing else."

"What the hell was that?" Vriana exploded.

"He's a reader," Pete said. He rubbed absently at his temples.

"But all readers are regulated, the government..." she paused as the skin on Granny's face tightened.

"We don't discuss that," Pete said mildly. She gulped and nodded.

"Are you sure that's a true reading, Granny?" Pete turned back to the thin man.

"As true as it can be."

That told Pete little. It could be true but it could also be a block. Many times he'd used readers in his work, but he's always been careful to verify everything. Too many corporations and governments employed senders to muddy the information the readers would dig up. A kernel of truth could be hidden in what Granny had said but there was no way to be sure.

Unless Pete metamorphasized into some inhuman monster.

A sneeze itched at his nose. He rubbed it. Already the lymph nodes on his neck were swelling. The cold, the virus, sure had a hold on him now. Monster. He suppressed a shudder.

Well, if he was going to do that, the least he could do was keep his mind from being sucked away by government scientists. He imagined Vriana felt the same.

"Okay Granny," he said. "That was the information. Now the passage."

"Hold on, Peter," Granny protested. "That took a lot. It's more than I give my paying clients."

"Consider it your payment," Pete said.

Granny's hands twitched as if he wanted to pull out the handkerchief and wipe them. When he settled for rubbing them on his pants legs, Pete knew he'd won.

Against the light from the wall screen, Vriana's face took on a greenish glow. Pete wondered briefly if the virus caused changes in skin colour, then shook his head. There was no sense in being morbid.

Granny hunched over the keyboard, staring at the display. His skin colour looked positively putrid, but that was an improvement as far as Pete was concerned.

"Not that way," Granny murmured. He plucked at the keys. "Lord, Peter, what the hell did you do? You've got warrants all over the place."

Vriana's face tightened and Pete felt himself frown. Dammit, they had to get out fast before the net closed in. Maybe, just maybe, pissing Spike off had not been one of his smarter moves. He'd never thought her revenge would reach so wide.

"Okay, I think I have something," Granny said. "It's going to cost."

"Whatever," Pete said. He dug out a forged bank chip and handed it to Granny.

"It's a father-daughter, heading for Chile. I can reroute the tickets and give them your id."

"Daughter?" Vriana asked.

"Not gonna get anything better," Granny said.

"Good enough," Pete said. He had friends down in South Am. He and Vriana could disappear. He allowed a smile to touch his face.

"That'll do."

Vriana tugged at the collar of her style-of-life suit.

"Stop that," Pete hissed. His voice came out like a whine through the mask.

"This is so damned uncomfortable," she said.

"Not as uncomfortable as being shot in the head."

She released the collar. "Pete, could he be right about the virus?"

Even through the distortion of the filter, he could hear the fear in her voice. It touched a similar chord in him but he couldn't afford to let it resonate. He couldn't be distracted.

It was a job, that's what this was. He took a deep breath and his professional mask helped push the fear away. This was his last smuggle, the most important. No way would he blow it.

It was the only way to think about it, the only way to keep the memory of Wilson's death dance at bay. The only way to keep from wondering about Matrix. Had he been a red when they found him in Rosedale? Or a green? Pete's head ached dully and a cough tickled his throat. The damned virus, damned cold. Anger rose up to blot out the fear but neither emotion was useful. Being emotional meant he was concentrating on something other than the job, and this job, more than any other, was too important.

"It doesn't matter," he said. "We'll worry about the virus when we get out of here."

She stared at him for a moment and then nodded.

Just then the boarding call for their shuttle came over the loud speaker, almost unintelligible. Pete took Vriana's elbow and began steering her through the crowd, toward the gate.

He didn't know what made him look back, maybe nothing, maybe instinct, the same way he knew which officials to bribe and which not. He caught a flash of grey silver out of the corner of his eye. Amidst all these colours it was probably nothing, or it was cops.

In a split second, he knew and oddly, the knowledge took the fear away, leaving a sense of calm. He was a smuggler and the cargo was all important. The cargo, the woman whose arm he clasped. Warm and wild, strong enough not to need him. Not after this. Somehow that made it easier.

"Hold on to your ticket," Pete whispered to her. "Don't say anything. Keep looking straight. Go through the gate and get your seat. Remember to dump the ID when you land. Vriana, whatever you do, whatever you hear, don't look back."

And he released her arm.

She kept walking, the hard learned homeless discipline gave her that. Even when Pete broke and ran, trailing armoured-clad cops like bouncing marbles, she kept walking. As the hulking gorillas closed in, stunner sticks raised, he saw she'd taken his instructions to heart.

She did not look back.

Damn good smuggle.

The world turned black.

They must be approaching planet fall, the creature that had once been called Pete thought fuzzily. The hibernation units had started to hum an hour ago, slowly wakening their cargo. In his, Pete stretched, arm pairs unclenching. The unit was too small for him to stretch his many legs, so he kept them retracted. He realized he'd awakened first. He was always first to do something. When he'd begun to realize this, he pretended he didn't know or couldn't do it until later. That way his conditioning was less, that way they'd missed a few things.

A few things like he remembered what he'd been before, a smuggler, a human. The others didn't remember but after being in contact with him for a while, he noticed a slight spark of awareness alight in their many eyes. And this started him wondering.

He wondered exactly what the nature of this virus was, exactly how much mutation arose in the virus before it registered as a red. Was there a margin for error?

And slowly, since most thoughts came very slowly right now, he realized that maybe his greatest smuggle wasn't Vriana (whoever that was), but himself. Himself and this virus. This mutated virus.

And not a customs inspector for a billion miles.

Pete snuggled in his hibernation tank and waited for his fellows to awaken.

Face Dances

Nick had to smile when he thought of the police searching for a blond man with another face.

He'd made it into the park across the street moments before the first siren screeched like some prehistoric bird in the late afternoon. Running from tree to tree, he disposed of the wig easily enough, flash-frying it in a garbage can. The heat would confuse the police sensors, giving him another diversion. In those few critical moments he would be able to do something about his face.

The thick bush he finally found to hide in was some bastard pine hybrid. Sticky sap clung to his shirt as he crouched down, peering at the crumpled picture of a man's face printed from one of the numerous, anonymous catalogue disks he subscribed to. First he stared at that face, memorizing the lines, the tilt of the nose, then he looked into a small hand mirror. His current face stared back at him, different lines, a different tilt. Concentrate. Think about that catalogue face, that other face. He studied one then the other, one then the other. Slowly the face in the mirror shifted, changed, features melting and blending, becoming indistinct. Then they sharpened, changing to match the catalogue face, a perfect reflection.

Beads of sweat popped from his newly formed forehead, testament to his strenuous efforts. He rested a moment, catching his breath. But he couldn't rest for long. The police would still be looking for him, and although he looked sufficiently different for them to ignore him if one cop decided to be zealous about searching everyone he could be in big trouble.

After changing his clothes and flash-frying them in another garbage can, he tucked the withdrawal cubes into the waist of his pants. Now he was ready. He stepped out onto the path.

A blue sensor beam hit him full in the face. He swallowed his panic, forcing himself to stand still and relax. They couldn't know it was him, he wasn't in the bank long enough for them to get a DNA reading.

The beam switched off and a young cop lower his pulser gun. "Sorry sir, we're looking for a suspect. Have you seen this man?" He held up a holo cube and triggered the image.

Nick pretended to study it, frowning slightly for effect. "No, I'm sorry, I haven't seen anyone like that."

"Thank you sir. You'd better leave the park now." The cop moved away, holding his gun at ready. Nick took his advice and hightailed it out of there.

Riding the shuttle out of downtown, he smiled again, his hand stealing a pat at his waist. He hadn't had a chance to check the amount but he was sure the take was close to five hundred thousand. Not bad for a half hour or so, not counting the two months spent casing the bank and preparing.

Gotta love my face, he thought.

The next day, Nick spent three hours making the two kilometer trip across the city to see Benji. On the way, he changed his face three times, had lunch on a rooftop cafe, and picked up his makeup bag from a locker in the speedtrain station. Benji knew him as a master of disguise, assuming that he used makeup to effect his changes. Nick wasn't about to shatter the man's illusions.

Sitting on an old wooden chair, Benji was putting the finishing touches on a pair of leather moccasins when Nick walked in.

"Hey Bill," Benji called. He raised one large, thick knuckled hand in a wave. The chair groaned.

"Nice pair of moccasins," Nick said. "How long does it take you to make them?"

Benji shrugged and scratched at his crooked nose. Despite being able to afford having it straightened several times over, the man wore it like a badge of honour. Got it in his first bust, he always bragged. "Depends how much time I've got and how much heart. What's doing?"

"I have some pretty rocks for you." Nick set the bag down on the table beside Benji. Leaving the moccasins, Benji pulled the cord on a floater lamp hovering near the ceiling. Slowly it descended until Benji stopped it. Thick fingers fiddled with the bag. It took him a little while to open it but Nick didn't offer to help. Ever since they'd fused the nerves during his last bout of prison, Benji had had a hard time with fine finger movements. It spelled death to his career as a safecracker but Benji was not deterred. He'd become a clearing house, using the contacts acquired in his vast career to arrange the movement of certain acquired items. Making moccasins helped him keep his fingers working. Sort of.

Once the bag was open, Benji spent a few minutes studying the diamonds. A smile flittered over his ugly face.

"Lovely," he purred. "I'm glad you finally decided to part with these. I have people practically pissing their pants for them."

Nick smiled. "Eloquent as always, Benji."

They haggled over the cost, Benji grumbling before giving into Nick's price. He handed over the cash chits and stocks. As Nick tucked the bills safely into the waist of his pants, Benji waved one large hand at him.

"Hey, I heard something you might be interested in."

Nick was already thinking of a vacation with sun drenched sand. "Hmm?"

"Yeah, Dopler's coming out with a new chip, supposed to revolutionize the net. Lots of people interested."

"How interested?"

Benji's eyes twinkled. "Almost ten M's worth is how I hear it. If you're listening."

Nick was definitely listening. With ten million he could buy his own island down south and have enough change to live comfortably for a while. For quite a while.

"Dopler's based in Geneva," Nick said.

"Yeah, but the big cheese lives in Toronto, keeps his head office here, nice and cosy. Rumour has it the chip is here and will only be shipped for production when the announcement is made."

"What's the big deal with it?"

Benji shrugged, a lopsided movement of his massive shoulders. "Dunno, Bill, I never was a nethead but I know people who are and they're buzzing with it. Pressuring me for potentials. Of course I mentioned you."

Nick smiled easily. If he took the job and succeeded Benji got a nice cut for his reference. Easy money, minimal risk. Usually Nick was leery of reference jobs, too many times his risk was too high. But Benji had been on the frontline himself and knew how to gauge the potential, see all the hazards. He trusted Benji's judgment. As much as he trusted anyone's.

"I could be interested."

Benji nodded. "How about drinks at Rafe's, around eight?"

"Fine."

Benji smiled, his face twisting into a horrible grimace. "I'll set it up."

The line outside Rafe's Italian Restaurant was long, but when the maitre d' spotted him, Nick was quickly ushered inside. They bypassed the main dining room, heading down a dimly lit hallway. Nick's feet sank into the two inch thick carpeting. At a heavy, dark door, the maitre d' knocked, listened, then pressed his palm to the reader beside it. The door clicked open and with a bow, the maitre d' waved Nick inward.

The walls were papered with dark green velvet. Plush burgundy curtains framed windows shuttered with black steel panels. A wide black onyx table glistened beneath a single hoverlamp. In the corners of the ceiling Nick noticed small jammers hovering unobtrusively. The lights on their sides blinked a steady green.

From the shadows around the door, one of two large men clad in identical grey suits stepped forward. He pushed Nick's arms up and frisked him briskly. At the table, Benji, dressed in his best worn suit, struggled to his feet.

"Hey, I said Bill was okay."

Beside him, a thin, elegant man held up one perfectly manicured hand. "Merely a precaution, Benjamin."

Passing their inspection, the two men let Nick

take his seat at the table. Benji sat at his right, looking anxious, unsure from the controlled expression on Nick's face if there had been any insult. The elegant man beside Benji didn't look concerned in the least. He openly studied Nick with cool, grey eyes set in a pale face. Beside him, another man, black curly hair unmanageable on his head despite the obvious effort, hunched inside his black suit as if it were as uncomfortable as a suit of armor. Uncertainness reflected in his eyes, unlike the woman who sat in the final place at the table. Dressed in a long sleeved, forest green dress, she merely looked bored.

"Thank you for joining us, Mr. Levine," the elegant man said. "I am Mr. Brantford. My associates Mr. Cresswell and Ms Drier."

Cresswell bobbed his head, curly hair spilling farther on his forehead. Ms Drier sipped her wine without looking at him.

"You're looking to acquire a particular item," Nick said to Brantford.

Brantford smiled, his mouth full of perfectly straight, white teeth. False, Nick thought, possibly temporary for this meeting, like the smooth, plastic-looking skin of his face giving him non-descript features. Must be high up in the computer world if he was this cautious about being recognized in a place so renowned for secrecy.

"A very particular item, Mr. Levine." Brantford lit a cigaretto, blowing smoke up toward the hoverlamp. The paleness of the smoke matched his hair, Nick thought, he must be almost albino. At his gesture, one of the thugs filled Nick's glass with a red liquid. One sip and Nick's eyes widened. Real wine, not the synthetic stuff. Brantford and his friends had a lot of money.

"Dopler Technologies has developed a new chip which is poised to revolutionize the industry," Brantford said. "It would place them head and shoulders above the rest of us and it would be years, possibly decades, before we could catch up. Such an imbalance would be disastrous. We want to get a copy of the chip to head off this situation."

"What's so special about this chip?"

Cresswell leaned forward, his elbows wrinkling the table cloth. "I don't think it's necessary for you to know that."

Nick turned an impassive look on Cresswell.

"If it has even the slightest impact on this job I have to know."

Cresswell flushed and slouched back in his chair. Beside Nick, the Drier woman chuckled. Nick glanced over at her. He'd assumed she was just Brantford's current appendage; now he wasn't so sure.

The albino man's expression was as impassive as Nick's. "The chip is a new development in nano technology. My intelligence tells me it's partially organic."

Nick's eyes widened. Organic. He began to understand Brantford's concern. An organic chip would be self sufficient, would be able to repair itself, to distinguish between useful and harmful tampering, could possibly even begin to change itself, acquire new pieces. Learn.

Maybe it would become conscious.

A conscious computer chip would know all the tricks, would be able to infiltrate any normal database with ease.

Brantford nodded. "I see you comprehend what this means." He glanced over at the woman. She nodded.

Nick looked over at her, studying the round, pale face framed by dark hair pulled back into a roll. Green eyes, heightened by the colour of her dress, looked at him. Did he detect a hint of amusement in them?

"We believe you are right for this job," Brantford said. "We've already decided on when it should be done. We just need one more person."

Finally Nick turned back to him. "One more person?"

"It's a two person job," she said. Her voice was a deep purr.

Her full name was Casey Drier, he learned, and she was an expert at disguises. Almost as good as Nick, she claimed. As they worked on the job, Nick began to wonder if Brantford's plan was the best. Stealing the chip in the middle of a full blown reception seemed inordinately risky but after studying Dopler's movements he begrudging agreed.

"I'm glad you're beginning to see it our way," Casey said one evening. She lounged against the arm of the sofa, swirling wine around her glass. "Dopler has body guards up to his eyeballs. The only time he loosens up is at his receptions. I bet he even screws with them hanging around. I wonder what his wife thinks about that?"

"Maybe she asks them to join in. Are you sure these are the most recent plans?"

He scrolled through the building plans hologram hovering over his desk. Casey set her glass down on the coffee table and walked over to stand beside him.

"These show the most recent renovations here and here." Her hand moved through the ghostly walls which lit up green when her fingers touched the part she wanted.

"That means there's only three entrances, including the main ballroom/courtyard. These two will be locked and watched. I think our only way out is through the main one."

Casey sat down at the table. "That means walking through the reception. Is that a good idea?"

He glanced over at her. Her expression was slightly worried, a significant display for her. He'd learned quickly that she parceled out her expressions as carefully as he did.

"Going out either of the other two exits would raise questions," he said. "We're using Dopler to get us in, once we discard him, we can't be sure there won't be a DNA sampler at the exit, or even a palm reader. I won't have time to copy those things."

"Why would he have those precautions on the way out?"

Nick smiled. "We've been watching him for three months and you ask that? I think he's paranoid enough."

She looked unhappy but she nodded. "Okay, Bill. Let's go over the wife again."

The hologram popped up displaying Mrs. Dopler. She wore a chic silver and grey suit, collar upturned in the latest fashion. Nick had to admit that Casey had roughly the same build but their faces were a study in contrasts. Where Casey's nose was thin, Mrs. Dopler's was large and bulbous, where Casey's cheekbones were well defined, Mrs. Dopler's were flat, where Casey's lips were lush and sensual, Mrs. Dopler's were thin and defined. Some of Casey's features could be built up but would it be enough to convince the husband?

The door opened and Cresswell slipped in, brushing moisture from his curly hair. He cursed lightly.

"Damn rain, why don't they schedule it for night?"

Nick snorted with amusement as Cresswell shrugged off his coat. He hung it on a hook by the door where it promptly fell to the floor. He ignored it.

Moving to the table, he peered at the holo. "That the wife?"

Nick thought he looked like a badger, the way his face wrinkled up, making his nose look even bigger. But that was probably an over-estimation of his intelligence.

"This is the full body holo," Casey said. "Did you get a close up of her face like I asked?"

Cresswell reached into the pocket of his rumpled trousers. He flipped a projection cube at her. "Knock yourself out."

Casey caught it easily. "I'm going to try out

her look." She headed across the room toward the bathroom.

"And Dopler?" Nick said.

"Fredrick Johanson Dopler," Cresswell said. "Born in '98 in New York, just before the housing riots. His mother was one of the organizers and they spent most of his childhood dodging the National Guard. He emigrated to Toronto in '14 when he was a teenager and got drafted into the Compuwars. After that, he started working on network security, building up a reputation in the industry for his nearly impenetrable data bases. The Q chip is his most recent achievement."

"Q chip?"

"The nano chip. He's been working on it for almost three years."

"Did you get anything more on the chip itself?" Nick asked.

Cresswell shook his head, black curls bobbing around his ears. "The security around that chip is tighter than a virgin's ass. You know as much as we do."

Nick flicked off the holos. The glow faded, leaving the slick surface of the table. Deceptively slick, its black depths hiding the complex machinery of the holo displayer. Nick wondered if it was the only deceptive thing in the room.

"So basically all we really know are rumors," he said, leaning back in his chair. The leather molded around the muscles of his back. "I guess I'm wondering why you're going to all this trouble for a rumour?"

Cresswell stiffened. A flush rose in his cheeks turning the skin a blotchy red. "What the fuck is that supposed to mean?"

Nick's expression hardened. "It means I don't believe you when you tell me you don't know anything else, you little shit. My ass is the one on the line and unless you want to find somebody else to do the job, you'd better start talking."

Cresswell's hands knotted into fists. Nick leaned forward, tensing his legs, getting ready in case Cresswell decided to make a big mistake.

"Boys," Casey's voice interrupted. "Why don't you give the testosterone a rest?"

Both men turned to look at her. Nick's eyes widened in surprise.

"So what do you think?" Casey said.

She looked exactly like Mrs. Dopler.

It couldn't be makeup, Nick thought. He kicked at a pile of sludge on the foot path. The rain had stopped in the late afternoon, leaving behind the smell of wet earth and squished worms. The park was empty except for the sound of water dripping off the trees and the sucking sound of Nick's shoes on the muddy path.

If it wasn't makeup, what the hell was it? He didn't allow himself to think the thought but it snuck up on him in spite of his defenses. The clues were there, every time he'd seen her, the way she looked, just a little different, her cheekbones shifted, her nose a little sharper, her eyes wider. Like she was taunting him the whole time, daring him to ask, daring him to wonder.

An expert at disguises.

Who was she?

He'd never met anyone else who could do what he did. Of course, how would he know? The thought brought a dry chuckle.

Where had she come from? He'd done just

enough research to know that his ability to mimic other people's facial features had to be genetically engineered. He'd stopped short of trying to find out who and where. Calling attention to himself could be a big mistake. Several conclusions became obvious; if his ability had been designed, somehow he'd been taken, stolen, from the designers and placed in an anonymous Central Home, to grow up orphaned and unclaimed, just another ward of the state. Not exactly the future his designer had envisioned, Nick thought. He could imagine what they were looking for: the perfect spy, the perfect double. Of course to control him they would have to devise something to keep him loyal. He avoided imagining what.

She had to be another one, like him. How else could she affect those minor changes? She must do them automatically, he thought, they were so subtle no one else would spot them. Most people would see them but incorporate them into what they thought she looked like without really noticing. But he'd spent his whole life watching faces. Her subtle shifts where like flashing signs to him.

The real question was why did she do it? He maintained his face in its look rigidly, not allowing any kind of fluctuation for fear that someone might notice. Why would she take that risk?

How could he find out?

And where did the job fit into this? Did Brantford know about her ability? Cresswell didn't, the man was a flunky and not a very good one, he thought with scorn, but Brantford was too hard to read.

Was it possible that the man not only knew about Casey, but knew about Nick as well?

How could that be? And how was he going to find out?

"I can get you an easy twenty for these, Bill."

"That's good, Benji, I'd like it by midnight."

His brow wrinkled. "Why so fast? You're going to have plenty in a few days. More than you can spend in a lifetime."

"As long as the job goes well."

"Of course the job'll go well, these guys are pros. I wouldn't set you up with anybody else, you know that. Sure it's risky as hell but it's a hell of a lot better than those banks and jewellery stores. You'll never have to do a little job like that again, never have to risk some zealous cop with a grudge and a pulser gun."

"It'll set you up nicely too."

"Sure, but I wouldn't risk you if I didn't think it was legit. You and me are friends, Bill."

Yeah, we're friends, Nick thought on the way home. Or as close to friends as he'd ever gotten. It wasn't Benji he was uneasy with.

At the final briefing yesterday Casey had sat beside him as they studied the plans of the reception hall. Brantford had smuggled someone in wearing a pinhole high def camera with special sonar attachment for proper depth perception. Nothing substantial differed from the plans he and Casey had been memorizing but both watched intently anyway.

"It's Dopler's habit to present any new advancement himself," Brantford said. The smooth skin of his cheeks glistened in the sunlight streaming in from the transparent wall on his left. "Partly it's his arrogance and partly it's his paranoia, but it works to our advantage. At any suggestion, he'll want to take a look at the chip again."

On Nick's right, Casey shifted in her seat. Nick glanced at her covertly. Her dark hair fell in waves past her face, past her perfectly sculptured cheekbones. Her green eyes looked a little bit wider today.

"Tomorrow afternoon, Mrs. Dopler is going to the hairdresser in preparation for the reception," Brantford continued. "That is where we will make the switch. According to my information she will be at 900 Yorkville, Salon de Andre at five pm. Casey, I would like you to be there at four."

She nodded.

"The bodyguard?" Nick asked.

"We'll take him there," Brantford said. "William, you will be replacing him until you get into the reception and Dopler gets close to the chip."

Nick leaned back, listening to the finalization of the details. They'd gone through this before, he knew them by heart. He watched Casey. Her hands rested lightly on the table as she leaned forward, listening to Brantford. Her expression was all business, definitely a professional, no matter what else she was. Normally Nick would be pleased to work with her, but there were too many questions hovering in his mind. And Brantford. The albino man was smiling now, looking well pleased.

Too smooth, Nick thought.

So he'd prepared. It was too late to pull out, doing so would ruin his reputation. He'd never get another contract like this again. But he didn't just take their word. His own contacts verified how coveted the chip was. With a new face, a new set of ID, he may be able to make this job pay off more than even Benji had expected.

Sorry about this, Benji, he thought, but I have to cover my own ass. He knew the ugly con would understand that sentiment.

The Salon de Andre was deserted at four. Casey sat in the backroom, staring out a window, nervously rubbing her cheek. Nick shifted uncomfortably in his suit, fibra-steel of gun-metal grey with metallic sheen, stiff with bullet protectorant. It was especially warm with the tuxedo beneath.

He tugged at the collar. Why couldn't bodyguards spend the extra money and get the flexi-suits? he wondered.

"Is she here yet?" Casey asked for the fifth time.

"Not yet," Nick said. He watched the profile of her face. Today her nose was a shade sharper.

"How did you get into this business?" he asked.

She turned to look at him, surprised. It was the first time she'd looked at him today. "Are you kidding?"

He shrugged. "Just passing time." He pretended to study his shoes, aware she was still looking at him.

"The money," she finally said. "I needed some. A lot."

For what? he wondered. He looked back at her round face. Had she paid to have this done to her, could it be done that way?

"You have a lovely face," he said.

She stared at him, lips parted slightly but her jaw was clenched. He watched the muscles flex.

Behind him the door slid open. Cresswell's voice said: "She's here."

Taking Mrs. Dopler and the bodyguard proved easy. They waited until she was getting her hair shampooed before moving in. Nick listened to her struggle from the back room. Casey sat at the window, staring at her hands.

After five minutes of silence, Cresswell popped his head in. "We're ready."

Casey looked up. "I need some time to do up my face."

Nick turned back to her.

"Why don't you go get yourself ready as the bodyguard, Bill," she said. Her tone allowed no measure for argument.

He stared at her until the door slid shut, cutting off the view of her round, perfect face. He could have sworn he saw her cheeks flattening even as he watched.

Cresswell led him to the small change room where the bodyguard lay unconscious.

"I had them bring up your things," Cresswell said. He gestured to the small case beside the door. "Need anything else?"

"Just privacy," Nick said. He looked pointedly at Cresswell.

Blotches of red rose in his skin. "Fine," he sneered. The door snapped shut behind him.

Nick bent to make sure the guard was really out, then opened his case. He moved the makeup around to make it look like he'd used it then sat back on his heels. He stared at the guard. His face was wide, strong chin, thin nose at the bridge, widening to sharp, distinct nostrils. His lips were thick. No cheekbones to speak of on his fleshy face. Long delicate eyelashes brushed Nick's thumb as he lifted the eye lid to check the eye colour. Brown.

He stared at the face. Concentrate. See the features, the chin, the nose, the cheeks. Feel them. He breathed deeper, deeper. His heart beat faster. His mouth dried out. Concentrate.

As always, he felt the first change in his cheeks as a tingling sensation, like a sleeping foot being shaken away. Pain shot through the odd sensations of muscles flexing, moving, shifting. He felt his jaw stretching, widening. The joint cracked with a loud pop. He whimpered in his throat, the only sound he could make now. His lips were not yet finished.

He closed his eyes. Concentrate. Sharp tingles

in his eyelids, shooting down his nose. His nostrils itched like crazy. His gums blazed. The skin on his forehead stretched until it felt like it would snap.

His shaking hands dug into his thighs. His heart beat a ragged rhythm in his chest. Finally the tingling faded and all he felt was the thin sheen of sweat trickle down his cheek.

When he looked in the mirror, he saw the reflection of the bodyguard.

"You look wonderful, darling," Dopler said to Casey. He didn't even look at her.

"Thank you, dear," Casey said. She looked just like Mrs. Dopler, her hair upswept in a band of curls around the top of her head. By the office door, Nick stood with his hands folded in front of him. His expression was impassive.

"Shall we join our guests, dear?" Casey asked.

Dopler rubbed the bald spot on his head. "Yes I... yes." He took her arm, straightening his purple tie with the other. "We might as well have some of the food we're paying for."

He led her down the wide stairs, Nick

following discreetly. The carpeting reminded him of the lush carpeting at Rafe's. But here the object was not secrecy. He'd noticed the proliferation of cameras and sensing equipment when they'd "returned" from Mrs. Dopler's hair appointment.

"When is the presentation, dear?" Casey said. Her voice drifted back to him.

"At eight." Dopler looked at his watch. "God, it's almost seven."

"Maybe we should take one last look at the chip, dear, just before we eat."

Dopler's hand fluttered like some deranged bird. "Yes, let's do that."

At the bottom of the stairs, instead of turning right into the ballroom, Dopler led them to the left. Dopler pressed his palm to the lock and punched in a code. At the prompt, he said: "Three."

They followed a narrow hallway, brightly lit. Cameras stared at them, imbedded into the ceiling every five feet. Nick felt the tingle of alarm barriers across his waist. He knew they even had weight sensors in the floor and in the ceiling. Without the proper clearance by Dopler anyone entering this hallway would be stopped in seconds. Nick didn't want to think about how.

When they reached the door, Dopler took several minutes to open it. Finally it slid open, several inches of steel grating along the groove of the doorframe. The room beyond was small, barely ten feet across. Nick felt a chill run up his spine. The temperature was a precise fifteen Celsius, the optimum temperature for the chip. In the centre of the room, a pedestal stood at waist level. A clear box sat on top, a row of lights blinking, maintaining correct pressure, correct temperature. Inside, the chip floated suspended in clear fluid, cushioning the delicate membranes from damage.

Nick watched Dopler's face. The tension around his eyes melted as the man gazed at the chip. Wrinkles on his forehead smoothed over. The slight frown of nervousness faded. The constant twitching of his hands stopped and his gestures became fluid.

"See, my darling," he said. "Here is such incredible potential. It's just the beginning, a fledging of the new computer, the new real artificial intelligence."

"It is incredible," Casey agreed. "Take it out of the box please, dear. I can't see it through the liquid."

Dopler looked confused. "But it's clear."

Casey rubbed her eyes with her fingertips. "It must be the hairspray. Everything's been fuzzy since I left the hairdresser's. I do so want to see it clearly, dear. Your real triumph."

Dopler smiled, his thin chest puffed out with pride. "Of course, darling."

His carefully groomed fingers punched out the codes on the keyboard. The row of lights flashed once then blinked off. A soft click sounded and with a hiss, the lid of the box opened.

Now, Nick thought. He touched his belt. Casey stepped toward Dopler. Her hand casually touched his left arm, just as a wife might touch her husband. Nick snapped the projector from his belt and triggered it. Dopler stiffened as he felt the pin prick of the needle in Casey's palm. He didn't have a chance to utter a sound, the sedative was immediate.

"Help me with him," Casey whispered, too low for the audio sensors to pick up. Nick set the projector by the wall and stepped forward. Together they lowered the man to the floor. Dopler's eyes were closed. His chest rose and fell rhythmically.

Now was the tricky part. They hadn't counted on the hallway being so filled with cameras. Nick had been planning to send Casey out to watch for any signs of guards. But it wouldn't look right. The scene the projector was broadcasting to the room cameras showed Mrs. Dopler here in the room. She couldn't be in the hallway as well.

Nick stripped off the guard's suit, revealing the copy of Dopler's tuxedo. He crossed to the box, lifting the lid. The supporting fluid was cool and smooth on his fingers. The chip, barely the size of a mint, fit easily on the end of his index finger. All this fuss for something so tiny, he thought. He slipped it into the carrier box and then slipped the box into his pocket.

He turned back to Dopler. Casey was kneeling by him, loosening his shirt so he could breath easier. She looked up at him, a questioning expression on her Mrs. Dopler face.

"Do you have your stuff?" she whispered.

No way out now, he thought. He knelt across from her. "I don't need it anymore than you do."

Her mouth opened, shock making her cheeks tremble. Her features slipped a little.

"Careful," he whispered. "Pay attention."

Her hand went up to her chin and her features steadied themselves. Shock was still evident in her eyes, echoed by fear. "How?"

"You have a bad habit of shifting things a little."

"I... I didn't think anyone would notice."

"No one else would."

She didn't say anything else. She pointed at Dopler.

Nick looked down. The man's face was peaceful. Wide nose, thin chin receding into his neck. Concentrate. Nick took a deep breath and began.

Three minutes later he finished. He sat back on his heels, mopping his new forehead with a handkerchief. Casey smiled and nodded toward the door.

As they passed the projector, Nick triggered the second program, the one showing the guard staying by the door as Mr. and Mrs. Dopler left. Casey threaded her arm through his and they entered the hallway.

With each step, Nick grew more confident. The tricky part was over. All they had to do was get through the reception. Cresswell was waiting in a car by the front door. Everything was going according to plan. Nick suppressed a smile; not necessarily their plan.

They entered the ballroom. Music wove through the crowd. Elegant women and dapper men stood in groups, chatting, laughing, eating. Nick felt the chip in his pocket, Casey's hand on his arm. His gaze swept the crowd, searching. Yes, there was a good one, a third of the way in. Another few minutes and he and Casey would part company. Too bad, he thought, he liked her. Who knew what they could have done together. But he didn't feel like sharing. He took a step in, leading Casey.

"Nick," her voice whispered in his ear. "I have something to tell you."

Surprised, he turned to her. How did she know his real name?

"You're under arrest, Nick," she said.

Her right hand held some kind of projectile gun.

He lunged away, pulling her off balance with her hand still on his arm. Her first shot went wild, hitting a man on the arm. He yelled, his arm freezing into an upraised position. Nick was already running when he saw it. Oh my god, he realized, it was some kind of muscle freezer. She meant to freeze his face!

But he was already primed for his planned betrayal. As he dodged through the crowd the tingling was already starting, his muscles already shifting. He held the imagine of the face he'd picked in his mind's eye, careening off people as he ran. Ahead of him, he could see the doors opening. Police in riot uniforms streamed in.

He'd never make it to the door, Nick realized. They would search everyone for the chip, even if he did manage to change his face. His heart pounded. He'd be sent away, probably to isolation to prevent him from ever seeing anyone's face again.

He wouldn't, couldn't, let that happen. He still had one idea left.

Behind him, Casey's gun spat again and he felt a prick hit his jaw. He screamed, knocking into a woman in a green dress. Pain flared across his face, drowning out the tingle of his shifting muscles. He stumbled, falling to his knees. His eyes watered, blurring the image of the marble tiles in front of his hands. His left hand fumbled for the box in his pocket, grabbed the edges. One idea left...

The next thing he was aware of was Casey's hand on his shoulder. His eyes were still tearing madly and she handed him a handkerchief. Wiping his eyes, he saw she was still wearing her Mrs. Dopler face. The expression was stricken.

"You shouldn't have tried to run, Nick," she said. "It wouldn't have ended like this if you hadn't."

Two police officers helped him to his feet, securing his hands behind his back with plasti-cuffs.

"What are you talking about?" he asked her.

"After two minutes the effect becomes permanent. The antidote won't work." She gestured at one of the officers. He handed her a mirror and she held it up for Nick to see.

His face was a disaster. His eyes stared out of the ruin of a nose, flat and warped to one side, cheeks shifted impossibly, the jaw contoured at an angle, his left brow visible, the other one folded into his forehead. Grotesque, a face for the freakshow.

Nick started to laugh.

"Here's the box," one of the officers said. He handed it to Casey who flipped it open and then looked at Nick, puzzled.

"Where's the chip?"

"What chip?" he said, with a chuckle. "I didn't have any chip. You don't have any proof of me taking any chip, only of me impersonating someone. Maybe conspiracy but I believe that was a set up and won't hold up in court. That's all you have, Ms Drier, or whoever you are."

Casey's Mrs. Dopler face hardened. "Where's the chip?"

Nick shrugged against the two police officers as they began to steer him away. "Haven't seen any chip," he called to Casey. "But I suggest you try those hors d'oeuvres. They taste delicious." He swallowed elaborately.

His last glimpse of her was the dawning expression of awareness. Her mouth opened, eyes widened in surprise. Not a bad expression, he thought, even on Mrs. Dopler's ugly mug. But he had to admit, he preferred Casey's original.

Such a lovely face.

1 Of The Beholder

Delin Sabin Umlar coughed, rubbing dust from his eyes. Five minutes before, this room had been a normal holding chamber, off white walls, grey tiles of interlocking plasti-steel, the door as thick as the length of his hand. The explosion had torn out the door like a piece of paper, ripping it off its hinges and imbedding it in the opposite wall. Two of the guards had been crushed by the door; Umlar remembered seeing their bodies on the way in.

"We think she had a mega-gun," the sergeant said. He shook his head. "She was thoroughly searched. Don't know how we missed it."

"You'd miss it if she wanted you to," Umlar said softly. He snorted away dust and walked along the far wall, one hand trailing along its rough surface. With the sergeant hanging around, he couldn't get an accurate reading but it didn't make much difference. There wouldn't be anything useful.

"We're holding all transports in dock," the sergeant said. "She won't get off base."

Umlar smiled to himself. That would be inconvenient for the transports, stuck at a tiny way station in the middle of the Bolariano Nebula, the middle of nowhere. But he couldn't release them now. After almost three years hunting her down, he wasn't about to make the mistake of underestimating her again.

"Your cameras caught the escape," he said.

"Oh yeah," the sergeant said. "Recorded about twenty seconds worth then quit. Damn things always on the fritz. Too old, but they won't give us the money to replace them. Budget cuts."

The sergeant grumbled but Umlar ignored him. Twenty seconds. Getting better. Last time it had taken her almost a minute to disable the camera. It made him wonder, not for the first time, or the hundredth:

What were they going to do once they caught her for good?

He pushed that thought from his mind. He wasn't a judge or jury, his job was only to find her and take her into custody. Then she was somebody else's problem. And he would find her. He'd found everyone he'd ever hunted. A perfect record, not a blemish. Until her. He clenched his fists and turned back to the sergeant.

"How many ships have you got docked?"

"Almost seventy. Busy time of year."

Umlar nodded. "Let's get started."

A compliment of ten guards followed him to each ship but Umlar didn't let any of them aboard. He would go alone, boarding after the crew had left and been positively identified as themselves. They couldn't take any chances. She could fool the men, possibly even fool the machines, the retina scanners, DNA readers, fingerprint filers, but she couldn't fool Umlar.

Umlar had trained at the finest Academies,

been privy to the mysteries of the Single Oneness. Joining the elite Tele-Hunters Mission, he'd sweated over numerous exams, readings and scans before he was deemed worthy. He'd endured the facial tattoos, old ink ones injected with ancient bamboo shoots. He was a Hunter One and she was an untrained renegade. An abomination to everything he believed in.

Before the first ship, Umlar paused, orienting himself, performing the Trinsu exercise, realigning himself in the universe, in reality. He closed off the echoes radiating all around him and focused only on her, only on the one reading of her he'd managed to find, the only clear picture he'd ever found.

Young, maybe ten, brown hair too long, hanging in her face. Eyes staring in horror at the woman fumbling with the door lock. Pounding from the other side, harsh voices calling through the door. The woman rushing forward, scooping her into her arms. The woman's crying more frightening than the pounding and harsh voices. She struggles in the woman's arms. "Run," the woman whispers, but her mouth doesn't form the words, doesn't need to, the girl knows already what she would say. But fear makes her hesitate. The pounding, louder now, dents appearing in the door as they start to batter through. The woman finds her voice and screams: "Run!"

Over ten years running now, seven others tracking her before him, burning out before they caught her. He'd managed to catch her once. Her escape then had left an even bigger mess.

She wouldn't escape this time.

One final, deep breath and he stepped inside the ship. Long metallic corridors stretched ahead, lined with seams like badly made trousers, dull and grim as only transport ships could be. The lighting was too dim for his eyes, but he wasn't looking with his eyes.

Emptiness, no life echo. Scanning the crew, he was able to block any of their echoes in the ship. That would leave only her, only him. He slowly tracked through the corridors, the cramped living spaces with worn metallic hammocks, the work stations cluttered with tools and disks. He extended throughout the ship, seeing, hearing, smelling, willing himself along every surface but he couldn't see her.

Not here.

One ship down, sixty-nine to go.

They proceeded methodically, the sergeant's men adapting quickly to the routine of closing off the area around each ship's docking coil, transferring the crew for identification and holding until Umlar scanned the inside of the ship.

Empty.

Afternoon dissolved into night. Umlar wolfed down a nutribar and dry swallowed some energy pills. A headache pounded through his temples down his neck, hunching his shoulders. Even the relaxation exercises didn't help. He was pushing, getting close to the edge, but he couldn't stop now. Even a rest as short as half an hour could be crucial. He didn't want to risk her breaking through the net they'd cast. If she escaped into space he'd be back to square one.

"The next ship is ready, sir," the sergeant said, his normally smooth face lined with tension. Umlar nodded, rubbing absently at his temples, distorting his facial tattoo.

"Let's go."

The crew filed out, grumbling about the delay, glaring at the guards and at Umlar with unrepressed hostility. Glancing at him, their hostility was lined with fear; he saw it glowing around them in shades of yellow. They knew who he was, recognized the ritual tattoos on his cheeks, imbedded so deeply no laser could erase them without horribly disfiguring his face. They were his shield, his badge of honour, protecting him from the fearful, ignorant masses that never bothered to try to understand him.

The sergeant finished checking the crew off his log. "All here," he told Umlar.

They completed the identity verification and Umlar slowly scanned each of them. They were who they said they were, a normal transport crew, tired and annoyed at being holed up in the middle of nowhere while some arrogant telepath scoped through their brain, invading their privacy...

Umlar shook his head, disengaging from the slouching hulk of a man who stood before him. The hostility was draining after a while and he couldn't afford to be drained. He wondered if he should risk another energy pill.

The sergeant tapped the vid displayer. "Inside looks empty."

Umlar smiled. He'd caught the slight emphasis in the sergeant's voice. Looks empty. That didn't mean anything. With a grunt, he grabbed hold of the air lock and hoisted himself inside.

Another endless corridor, drab and dull. He'd seen so many corridors he'd be dreaming them for weeks. His steps echoed down the emptiness, reflecting the faint echoes of the crew. As he got more fatigued, Umlar found the echoes slipping past his barriers. He pushed them back, concentrating, remembering only her, only the girl.

He started at the bridge and worked his way back. The echoes of the crew were hardest to ignore in their quarters where every object resonated with their presence. He took several deep calming breaths, forcing the echoes to recede, his hands tracing the patterns of the Trinsu exercise in the air, focusing only on her, on the one echo he was looking for but hadn't yet found.

Leaving the last of the quarters, a small room packed with an impossible amount of stuff, he walked down the corridor toward the mess. Passing a secondary lift shaft, he glanced at it absently, and then caught something.

A smell, a scent, the barest whiff of an echo.

His breath stopped at the same time as his legs. Whirling, he stared at the shaft, concentrating until his lungs started to burn and he remembered to breathe. He took several deep breaths, trying to still his heart that thudded heavily in his chest. Concentrate.

There. There it was. An echo.

She was here.

He closed his eyes, fighting for control over his rising excitement. To get excited now would make him sloppy and if he gave her any chance she would plough right over him. Just as she had the others.

Quickly he checked the trancer at his belt. It was filled with the highest dose they could risk without killing her. It would bring her down, stop her from playing any of her tricks yet leave her coherent and responsive. One shot and she'd be easier to handle. The dose would last long enough to get her back to Earth, back to the probes.

He started down the shaft, focusing on the echo like a pinhole of light in absolute darkness. So faint, he almost lost it several times and had to climb up two levels before he caught it again.

Fourth level down. Engineering. Very smart, he thought, the most isolated part of the ship, yet still shielded.

The light was very dim, casting long shadows down the corridor. Umlar's own shadow was like a tiger melting into the brush as he inched forward, drawing the trancer in one hand, trailing his other hand along the wall.

The echo, still faint, led him on. He focused on it, feeling it resonate with his single scan of her. The last time he'd caught up with her, there'd barely been a time for a scan. This time he'd make sure he knew her, inside and out.

He came to one of the equipment rooms, filled with the debris of a hundred repairs. The echo was slightly stronger. He followed it inside, moving slowly into the room. He could barely see in the gloom. Four paces, five...

He spun and grabbed.

She jumped back with a cry, losing her footing. She crashed to the floor, landing hard on her rump. Her gun skidded away. She started to dive for it.

"Don't," he warned, leveling the trancer at her.

Her eyes were wider than he'd imagined and her brown hair was chopped to a few bristling inches on her head. She wore an ill-fitting space suit, probably "borrowed" from one of the crew.

"Why?" she said. She stared at the trancer.

"You're under arrest," he said formally, not that she needed to hear it, she knew that by now.

But her echo, instead of being calm and contained like he expected, bubbled with anger, pain and fear. Tears filled her eyes.

"Why?" she cried. "I haven't done anything wrong."

"I'd say the people you've killed would disagree with that."

"I was defending myself. I just want to be left alone, but you people keep chasing me. I haven't done anything."

She was quite young, younger than her years. Over half of her life running. And killing people along the way, he reminded himself.

"Did they even tell you why you're hunting me? Did they give you a reason? Or are you just like some dumb dog, point and you give chase."

Beneath the fear he heard the harshness in her voice. Her echo was tinged with anger.

"That's not my job," he said. He primed the trancer. Better deal with her quickly, the longer he delayed the more of a chance he was taking.

"Do you want to know why they want me?" she shouted. "They want me so they can shut me up because they don't want you to know that you could've been like me."

She nodded at the cold expression on his face.

"Yeah, I never went to any training facility. I never took any drugs to help me focus my wild talent. They don't control me the way they control you."

"They don't control me," he snapped.

"Wrong," she said. "They want you to believe that. They want you to believe that the pain, the nose bleeds, the seizures when you're fatigued are normal because you're stressing your brain. And then when you burn out at thirty, you're dead. But it's not normal. It's the drugs, it's the training. They want to keep you weak so you can't learn to be strong."

Her echo was stronger, rising like a flood and almost as irresistible. Her fear vanished, replaced by waves of anger and determination. His head pounded, resonating with the beat of his heart. The hand holding the trancer trembled, and he felt the first twinge of fear.

She was trying to control him!

"No," he hissed, the word torn from his lips. The hand steadied. His finger tightened on the trigger.

Suddenly the pressure of her echo was gone and he felt a tinge of sadness brush him like a soft breeze.

"I'm sorry," she said. "I thought I could convince you."

Her eyes, wide and honest, and her slight smile were the last things to fade.

His mouth dropped open as he realized she'd done something he'd thought impossible. She'd fooled a telepath. Fooled him with an image, like he was a child. He managed one step back before the bomb exploded.

Cleanup took the rest of the night. After sealing the air lock, the sergeant ordered the ship blasted away from the station in case of other bombs. The ship's crew was in an uproar, demanding compensation for their destroyed ship and cargo. The sergeant waved them onto a guard and retreated to his office.

The com displayer chimed as he sat down at the desk. The stern face of an HQ general stared out at him.

The sergeant played a copy of the tape recorded off the pin camera he'd planted on Umlar. The general sat quietly for a moment, tapping his finger on his chin.

"You're convinced the tape is genuine?" he asked.

"Yes, sir. Not even Investigator Umlar knew he was wearing it. There's no way she'd tell from a scan of him. It looks like she decided not to be taken alive."

The general sighed. "I want a full report and detain those ships until you can verify everyone on them. Just to be sure."

"Yes sir," the sergeant said. He saluted smartly as the general's image faded.

Leaning back in the chair, the sergeant took a deep breath. Shoulders slumped with fatigue, one hand came up to brush at the brown bristles.

Too bad. She hadn't wanted to cut off her hair. But it would grow back, once she left the station and became herself again. She smiled at the sergeant's pug face reflected in the dark surface of the displayer, watching the thin lips curl. Not such a bad face, she thought.

The door chimed and she stood up, ready to resume the sergeant's duties.

REAWAKENING

The room came slowly into focus, as if she were seeing it through a gauze curtain. Bare white walls. Anemic sunlight highlighted tiny cracks near the ceiling. The tang of disinfectant made her slightly nauseous. She tried to make her gaze follow the path of the sunlight but it only made her aware of the sluggish feeling in her body. Where? The thought barely formed in her mind before the hiss of a door distracted her.

"Welcome. Nice to see you're awake, J358," said a deep gentle voice.

With effort, she managed to turn her head. A tall, thin man wearing a dull white lab coat stood inside the door. He moved to the foot of her bed, lifted the tiny data bead from the recording stand and pressed it to the metallic patch on his temple.

"I see you're coming along quite nicely. Excellent. We'll have you ready for trial in plenty of time, J358."

She was in a hospital obviously but what had happened? "What happened?"

"I'm sorry I can't discuss that, J358. I believe the court officer will explain everything."

Now he was moving toward the door. She struggled to sit up but her weak muscles would not obey her.

"Wait, what court officer? Why are you calling me J358? My name is Janice."

He threw a pitying look back at her. "Not anymore."

The door hissed closed behind him, leaving her floundering. What did he mean 'not anymore'? What had happened to her and why couldn't she remember?

The strain exhausted her further. Fatigue overwhelmed her even as she tried to remember what was going on. The memory of dressing for work blurred and fragmented into vaguely disturbing dreams.

The next time she woke to find a dark haired woman dressed in a silver suit sitting by her bed. Lifting her head, Janice felt stronger. This gave her the confidence to glare at the woman.

"Who are you?"

The woman glanced up from her small box of data beads. "Ah, you're awake, J358. I am Natasha Montgomery from the fifty seventh district court and am assigned to prep you for trial."

Janice tapped the bed and it raised her to a sitting position. "What trial? What is going on? My name is Janice Belsom, not J358."

The court officer smiled, a vague expression that did not reach beyond her lips. "I'm sorry. The doctors are supposed to orient you before I arrive but they never bother." She sighed, as if this was another burden she had to bear. "You are not Janice Belsom. Janice Belsom was murdered six months ago. You have been cloned from her

DNA to provide testimony at the trial of her accused killer. Surely your originator heard of this procedure?"

Indeed she had and the thought of it made her ill. Using sophisticated energy bombardments, doctors had been able to measure and preserve personality within human tissue for DNA cloning. Soon real copies of people could be created but were deemed illegal under all but the strictest of circumstances. Testimony about your own murder was that circumstance.

"I was murdered," she mumbled.

"Your originator was murdered," Montgomery corrected. "You're going to testify at the accused's trial."

"But I don't remember anything," Janice said. "How can I testify?"

Montgomery nodded sagely. "You will. Memory loss of recent events is a common effect upon animation. You'll remember soon enough."

And she did begin to remember, as much as she didn't want to. Over the next several weeks as her strength returned so did her memory. Natasha Montgomery visited every day, supportive and attentive to her newly emerging memories but Janice knew the court officer saw her only as an important piece of evidence. Although Natasha addressed her as 'Janice', her tone implied 'J358'.

A month after her animation they moved her out of the hospital and into government lodging. Since she wasn't actually Janice Belsom she had no legal claim to her own belongings. No, she corrected, to her originator's belongings. The thought soured her throat.

Every day she opened her eyes expecting to see her own brilliant white bedroom, to feel the salty breeze off the ocean, to hear the soft hiss of the waves. Instead what greeted her was the dingy beige walls, the smell of grease and the sound of the recycling factories roaring to life. She awoke from her dreams to a nightmare.

The problem was she still felt like Janice, not like J358. She didn't know what an animated copy was supposed to feel like. No one could tell her. Nor was there anything for her to do except regain her memories and prepare for the trial. She tried not to think about afterward. She had heard about the policy regarding animated copies.

After the disastrous animal grown organ riots in '73, only real human organs were deemed legal, once again resulting in unacceptable shortages. Until animated copies became marked for "disposal and harvest" according to the Originator Purity Act in '75.

Janice tried not to be bitter, after all she was getting a chance to confront her killer. But she didn't want to die. She had too much to do.

Yet they wouldn't let her do anything, even when she requested materials to work on some sculpture, the court officer only looked amused.

"You don't have to work anymore, Janice," Natasha Montgomery said. "Just relax and remember, that's all you need to do."

So she remembered. Remembered the rain dripping off the overpass as she walked along the street. She'd left her personal shield at home, forgetting that rain was scheduled for that evening. Normally she wouldn't walk in the east end at that time of night without a shield but her client had been adamant. He had to have that particular type of steel in his sculpture and her supplier was only open in the evenings. The rotating laser lights had taken too long; the deadline now fast approaching. She hadn't any other choice.

The dripping rain was cold on her neck and smelled of smoke. Her wafer boots splashed in the puddles as she emerged from the overpass. The street was supposed to glow but naturally it didn't work in the east end. Not much did.

Only two blocks to her supplier's warehouse. She'd imagined his offices, dry and warm. A bottle of white wine chilling, some fresh bread and humus to warm her bones would be waiting as they discussed tensile strengths and negotiated prices. A faint smile had spread across her face when the man stepped out from behind her.

Janice usually stopped herself from remembering at that point but always snatches filtered through: the stench of his hand across her mouth, the pressure of his fingers on her throat, cold rain dripping off his hair and into her eyes. She'd tried to give him her credit numbers but it wasn't enough. His fingers pressed. Her throat contracted. Her mouth opened. Rain water dripped on her lips. No air...

"Natasha, can I get a room with a window that

opens?" she asked Montgomery one day. The court officer looked at her quizzically.

"Why do you want that?"

Janice crossed her arms. "It's too stuffy in here."

Montgomery's smile was smug. "Of course, Janice. Now I want to hear about the evening again."

Janice hated Montgomery's patronizing superiority, especially because it was so well hidden. Always polite, always attentive. Gently discouraging anything that had nothing to do with the trial, always the trial. Janice got so sick of it.

"When is the trial?" she asked.

"Starting soon," Montgomery said. "In a couple of weeks. You'll be testifying by the end of the first week. You'll finally get a chance to face the accused."

Janice stared out the window after the court officer packed up her data beads and left. Did it matter if she managed to face the accused? Her originator was dead. Where did that leave her? Her role was only to identify the killer, point a finger and say he was the one. Then she was finished and, like any other piece of evidence, was disposed of, her organs harvested. It wasn't fair. They'd scraped her off her originator's dead body, grown her in a lab and induced her memory just to convict a man in a trial. Yet she wasn't allowed to live her life, her originator's life. Wasn't that a crime in itself?

But she didn't have rights. Only someone who had rights could have a crime committed against them. The bitterness tasted like overcooked broccoli, flat and slimy.

The next day Montgomery strolled in with a suit bag over her arm. She laid it carefully down on the bed as Janice watched from her chair by the window. The court officer peeled back the cover to reveal a navy suit. It looked exactly like the ones Natasha Montgomery always wore, fashionable, chic and tasteful. Everything that Janice had never been. She was awkward, uncoordinated and cared not a whit for trends. Qualities that made her art unique and valuable. Qualities she was no longer allowed to express.

"This is for the trial," Montgomery said. "Try it on. I bet I got your size right."

Janice stared at her smirking face. Of course she'd gotten the size right, they'd grown her to order, hadn't they? Anger tightened her skin, made her scalp itch. Montgomery could have brought one of her originator's own dresses. A small courtesy, but the court officer hadn't bothered. And why should she when Janice wasn't really Janice, was only J358?

Montgomery's face clouded. "What's wrong? Don't you like the suit? It's new. It's a Flaherty."

"It's fine, Natasha," Janice intoned. With staccato movements, she jerked off the gray fatigues and dragged on the suit. The material scraped against her flesh and although the size was right, it felt wrong. It dug in under her arms and sagged at her waist.

"Do you like it?" Montgomery asked.

Did it really matter? Janice wondered. Even though she didn't would the court officer care enough to dig out one of her originator's dresses? Probably not. Montgomery would probably only consent to refigure the colour. A lot of difference that made.

"The suit's fine," Janice said.

Montgomery's smile blossomed, perfect lips stretching over perfect teeth. Janice wanted to rip off the suit and jam it down her throat.

"Terrific. Now let's go over your testimony, Janice. The trial is starting on Monday."

Janice's breath caught. "Can I watch?"

Montgomery shook her head. "I'm sorry you can't. It could taint your testimony. But you'll get a chance to face the accused soon enough. Now your testimony..."

After the session, Montgomery left the suit. Janice took it off to don the shapeless gray fatigues. They weren't anything like her old clothes but at least it wasn't the artificial style of the court officer's taste. She stared out at the gray streets. Maybe she could run away. For a moment, she indulged her fantasy, imagined escaping the drab government building, racing along the gray street, hopping on the nearest shuttle and heading back toward the ocean. She could find a small town, one of the ones with limited connectivity. They were all the rage now. She could make a living selling small sculptures to tourists. A smile touched her lips then faded. It was impossible. It didn't matter if she ran, they'd implanted a homing gene into her DNA. They'd just swoop in and scoop her up again. No escape. Janice sighed, closing her eyes.

Sunlight filtered through the windows of the transport. Janice peered out at the tall white building. All clean lines, easily delineated areas of shadow and light. The transport moved past the front, past the bored reporters waiting for entrance, and swung around the back. Naturally she couldn't go through the front, she thought, she wasn't a witness. She was evidence.

The suit scrapped against her legs as the door opened and she stood. Light spilled in, making her blink. She stepped down, ignoring the driver's offered hand.

So here she was, the trial had finally arrived. Her stomach tightened. Anxiety made it hard to breathe. She blinked in surprise. She hadn't expected to be upset. This wasn't about her, it was about her originator. She was only a copy. But it didn't matter how often she said it to herself, how often she saw the look in Montgomery's eyes, she still felt like Janice Belsom, and Janice Belsom was nervous.

Natasha Montgomery waited just inside the building. She motioned to Janice in a distracted way. Janice noticed the ear bug; the court officer was probably listening to the trial.

"Almost time," Montgomery said. She flashed an artificial smile. "Ready?"

"Sure," Janice said. What would happen if she said she didn't remember anything? Would they keep her around indefinitely? Or would they dispose of her and start again with another copy? Her breath stuck in her throat. Had they already done that? She gagged on the perfectly filtered air.

Montgomery took her arm firmly. "Are you all right?"

Janice wiped tears from her eyes. Her cheeks felt flushed. "I'm fine. Just nervous."

Again the artificial smile, too perfect and too bright. "You'll be terrific. Let's go."

Janice followed her down the drab hallway. Their footsteps didn't even echo, the floor absorbed them as if they weren't even there. Maybe she wasn't really here, she thought. Maybe it was a vivid dream and she would wake up soon. The large door in front of them slid open. Sounds of the trial spilled into the hallway, the murmur of the reporters, the scrape of chairs against the tile floor, the judge's droning voice. Harsh light made her blink as she stepped through the doorway. Montgomery stopped just to the right and motioned her forward. Janice knew she had to go forth on her own now and suddenly even the presence of the arrogant court officer would have been a comfort.

Her footsteps sounded overly loud after the muffled hallway. She could feel everyone staring as she advanced to the witness stand. It looked to be miles away. The judge frowned at her as she stumbled by. Finally her hand closed on the rail and she pulled herself into the seat. The suit bunched uncomfortably around her waist. Sweat trickled down her back. Would they swear her in? She wasn't really a witness.

As another court officer stepped forward, Janice finally looked across the room and saw the defendant. Her breath caught in her throat. It was him. Even with the dim light that night, she remembered his thin, angular cheeks, the way his nose listed to one side, the watery blue eyes glaring desperately into hers. He was all cleaned up now, his beard neatly trimmed and his wild hair combed down, but his eyes still held desperation, that she could see from across the room.

The prosecutor stepped forward, just as Natasha Montgomery had briefed her, and started taking her through that fatal night. As she listened to his questions, she started at her killer. No, her originator's killer. He didn't look nearly as horrifying as she remembered. He was a thin, short wisp of a man with trembling fingers, so desperate to stay alive that he had to kill to do it. But wouldn't anyone do that if they had to? Wasn't she desperate?

"J358, can you identify your originator's killer in this courtroom?"

Janice looked at the prosecutor, then back at the man sitting behind the defense table. It would be so easy to point at him, to do what they wanted, and it was the truth wasn't it? But did it matter? Did it bring her back, give her any more life? He would go to prison where he would be fed, clothed and sheltered for the rest of his life, and she would be disposed of because all she was was evidence.

"J358, answer the question please." The judge's voice barked at her.

Her nails dug into her palms. "I'm sorry," she said smoothly. "I don't recognize him here."

The courtroom erupted in noisy bedlam, the judge shouting for order. Through it she watched the desperation leech out of the defendant's eyes and be replaced by fear. He knew she recognized him and hadn't said it. He probably didn't understand why but she didn't care. She hadn't done it for him. Her relief even made the awful suit comfortable.

To hell with the truth, she thought. Maybe she was only evidence, but she was evidence they needed to keep around until they could get a conviction. She bit her lip to stop the smile from forming as Montgomery came to lead her away.

"You lied."

Janice turned away from the window and looked at the court officer. Natasha Montgomery's hands were clenched and her normally relaxed expression was tightened with rage.

"I testified the way I remembered it, Natasha," Janice said. "Sorry you didn't like what you got."

"You lied. He was the one. We both know it. What do you think you've accomplished? Do you think they won't convict him?"

"If they do, it'll be overturned on appeal. No way they'll disregard my testimony. I was there."

"No, you weren't," Montgomery snapped. "Your originator was there. You weren't. You think because we animated you to testify that you can lie and we'll just let you get away with it. Do you honestly think we'll let you live longer without a conviction? I'm going to report that you're defective and order a new animated copy. You'll be disposed of immediately."

She tucked her data bead box under her arm and turned to leave. Deliberately, Janice picked up the lamp on the table, stepped forward and smashed it down on the side of her head. Montgomery staggered. The data bead box crashed to the floor, shattering. Data beads spiraled across the floor. Montgomery landed on her ass and looked up, one hand going to her head. Her lips moved but Janice didn't stop to listen to any more words. She tightened her grip on the lamp and swung again. And swung again...

They caught up with Janice, just like she knew they would, but at least she made it back to the ocean. She listened to the crashing waves as the officer steered her toward the police car. She let the sight of the water fill her eyes as they drove off back to the city.

The room looked hazy as she opened her eyes. Daylight filled the space. Bright white walls and an antiseptic smell told her she was in the hospital. Why, she started to wonder but the hiss of an opening door distracted her.

"Welcome. Nice to see you're awake, N917," said a gentle voice.

N917 turned to look at the doctor. Somehow she recognized him; he worked in the government hospital animating copies of murdered originators.

"No," she whispered.

The doctor moved to the foot of the bed, lifted the tiny data bead from the recording stand and pressed it to the metallic patch on his temple.

"I see you're coming along quite nicely. Excellent. We'll have you ready for the inquest in plenty of time, N917." He turned away and moved to the door.

"No." She struggled to sit up but the effort exhausted her and she fell back as the door hissed closed behind him. "No, I'm not N917, I'm Natasha."

But he was already gone.

ABOUT THE AUTHOR

REBECCA M. SENESE weaves words of horror, mystery, contemporary fantasy, and science fiction in Toronto, Canada. She is the author of the contemporary fantasy series, the Noel Kringle Chronicles featuring the son of Santa Claus working as a private detective in Toronto. She garnered an Honorable Mention in "The Year's Best Science Fiction" and has been nominated for numerous Aurora Awards. Her work has appeared in numerous Holiday Hijinks anthologies including *Whimsical Winter Wonderland, Happy Holiday Historicals, Tidbits & Tinsel Tales, Haunted Holidays, Mistletoe Merriment, Crazy Christmas Capers*, and *Toy Trucks and Teddy Bears*. She has also appeared in *Home for the Howlidays, Pulphouse Fiction Magazine, Unmasked: Tales of Risk and Revelation*, the *Obsessions Anthology, Fiction River: Superpowers, Fiction River: Visions of the Apocalypse, Fiction River: Sparks, Fiction River: Recycled Pulp, Tesseracts 16: Parnassus Unbound, Tesseracts 15: A Case of Quite Curious Tales, Ride the Moon, Hungar Magazine, On Spec, TransVersions*, and *Storyteller*, amongst others.

FIND ME ONLINE

RebeccaSenese.com
RebeccaSeneseBooks.com

www.ingramcontent.com/pod-product-compliance
Lightning Source LLC
Chambersburg PA
CBHW021221220726
48287CB00016B/2631